ALL I SEE

Story by Cynthia Rylant

Pictures by Peter Catalanotto

ORCHARD BOOKS · NEW YORK · LONDON

A division of Franklin Watts, Inc.

Orchard Books, 387 Park Avenue South, New York, New York 10016.
Orchard Books Great Britain, 10 Golden Square, London W1R 3AF England
Orchard Books Australia, 14 Mars Road, Lane Cove, New South Wales 2066.
Orchard Books Canada, 20 Torbay Road, Markham Ontario 23P 1G6

Orchard Books is a division of Franklin Watts, Inc.

Manufactured in the United States of America   Book design by Mina Greenstein
The text of this book is set in 21 pt. Perpetua. The illustrations are watercolor painting, reproduced in
four-color halftone   1   2   3   4   5   6   7   8   9   10

Library of Congress Cataloging-in-Publication Data.
Rylant, Cynthia. All I see. "A Richard Jackson book."
Summary: A child paints with an artist friend who sees and paints only whales. [1. Artists—Fiction.
2. Painting—Fiction]   I. Catalanotto, Peter, ill.   II. Title.   PZ7.R982Al   1988   [E]   88-42547
ISBN 0-531-05777-1   ISBN 0-531-08377-2 (lib. bdg.)

To Scott Savage, who loves the light —C. R.

To Ginnie and Tony —P. C.

*T*here once was a man named Gregory who spent his days beside a lake painting pictures. He wore an old gray raincoat when he painted, and two brushes were tucked behind his ears. Sometimes as he worked he also whistled Beethoven's Fifth Symphony very loudly, waving his brush in the air through the exciting parts. Gregory's white cat lay beside him, sleeping through it all, the painting and the symphony.

When Gregory tired of working and whistling, he picked up his cat, climbed into a canoe, and paddled off down the lake.

He lay flat on his back in the bottom of the drifting boat, staring straight up at the sky.

A boy named Charlie who summered at the lake used to watch Gregory paint and whistle and drift in his canoe with his cat. Charlie had decided he was fond of Gregory, though they had never met.

One day when Gregory was out in his canoe, Charlie sneaked a look at the picture Gregory was painting.

Charlie was surprised by what he saw, by what Gregory had
painted as he looked at Charlie's lake.
But the picture made Charlie like Gregory even more.

So each day when Gregory drifted away, Charlie sneaked a
look. And each day Charlie saw the same thing: a blue whale.
Sometimes the whale was diving in deep water, sometimes it
was leaping up out of the water, sometimes it was upside
down. But it was always a whale.

And Charlie became fond of whales, too.

But one morning when Gregory was away, Charlie found nothing on the canvas. No painting. No whale. No picture for Charlie.

So while Gregory drifted far off down the lake, staring at the sea-blue sky and humming Beethoven's Fifth, Charlie picked up a brush.

While Gregory stroked his sleeping white cat, Charlie squeezed out some paint.
And while Gregory rested and hummed, Charlie painted.

He left his picture there for Gregory. Charlie was too shy, and afraid, to stay.

When he paddled back to shore, Gregory was astonished to find a painting on his easel. He was even more astonished to see himself in the painting, standing at the easel, white cat sleeping, and musical notes bouncing all over the sky.

Gregory sat and stared at that painting for a long time.

The next day when Gregory went far off down the lake,
Charlie again sneaked a look and again found no blue whale.
But this time, painted on Gregory's canvas were these words:
I LIKED THE PICTURE
Charlie picked up the brush. He was smiling and his
heart pounded as he painted:
THANK YOU
Again, he was too shy, and afraid, to stay.

The following day there was a new message:

So Charlie stayed. And when Gregory paddled back to shore, he wiped his hands on his old gray raincoat, shook Charlie's hand, and introduced Stella, his cat.

For many days after that, Gregory and Charlie were at the lake together. Gregory taught Charlie about shadows and light, about line, about drawing things near and things far away.

He also taught Charlie how to scratch Stella under the chin without getting clawed.

And, of course, Gregory allowed Charlie to paint. Charlie painted whatever he saw. He painted everything he saw, there on the lake.

Gregory did not paint at all during this time.

Then one day Gregory waited for Charlie with a gift. He
had brought for Charlie an easel of his own, and new brushes,
and new paints, and clean canvases.

They stood side by side then, that day, brushes tucked behind their ears, painting. Gregory painted a blue whale floating in seaweed full of tiny pink fish. Charlie painted whatever he saw.

And at the end of the day, Charlie finally asked Gregory why he painted only whales.

Gregory's face opened up into an enormous smile. He looked out across the water and he said, "It is all I see." He smiled for a long time.

Charlie, too, looked out across the water, and he knew
Gregory's whales were there somewhere. He also knew that
something was waiting for him, waiting to be seen and to be
painted.